TEAM ROCKET TRUCE

Based on the episode "Sweet Baby James"

ADAPTED BY TRACEY WEST

SCHOLASTIC INC.

New York Toronto London Auckland Sydney
Mexico City New Delhi Hong Kong Buenos Aires

No part of this work may be reproduced, stored in a retrieval system, or transmitted in any form or by any means,
electronic, mechanical, photocopying, recording, or otherwise, without written permission of the publisher.
For information regarding permission, write to Scholastic Inc., Attention: Permissions Department, 557 Broadway,
New York, NY 10012.

ISBN-13: 978-0-545-00073-4
ISBN-10: 0-545-00073-4

© 2007 Pokémon. 1997–2007 Nintendo, Creatures, GAME FREAK, TV Tokyo, ShoPro, JR Kikaku, Pokémon
properties are trademarks of Nintendo.

Published by Scholastic Inc.
SCHOLASTIC and associated logos are trademarks and/or registered trademarks of Scholastic Inc.

12 11 10 9 8 7 6   8 9 10 11 12/0

Designed by Henry Ng
Printed in the U.S.A.

First printing, March 2007

Poor Munchlax!

"*Munchlax...*" the chubby Pokémon moaned. It leaned against the back of a tree and closed its eyes.

Munchlax's Trainer, May, knelt by its side. May's little brother, Max, and her friends Ash and Brock circled around them.

"This doesn't look too good," Ash said. His little Electric-type Pokémon, Pikachu, sat on his shoulder. Pikachu looked at Munchlax with worried eyes.

"Munchlax has been like that for a few days now," May said. Her blue eyes looked worried.

Normally, Munchlax was cheerful. It was always running around, looking for food.

Max held out a PokéBlock to Munchlax. "Here, you hungry?" he asked.

But Munchlax just moaned and shook its head.

"Munchlax *must* be sick if it's passing up a meal," Ash remarked.

"Then we'd better get to a Pokémon Center right away," Brock suggested.

May frowned. She and her friends were traveling through the Battle Frontier. None of them had ever been there before. Right now they were on a hillside. There was nothing but grass and trees around them. May hadn't seen a Pokémon Center for a long time.

Max took out his PokéNav. The handy device would tell the friends where they were, and what was nearby.

"Let me look," Max said. He pressed a few buttons. "It says there isn't a Pokémon Center anywhere near here!"

May looked at Munchlax and felt like crying. At a Pokémon Center, Nurse Joy would know what to do. But May had no idea how to help her sick Pokémon.

"Now what are we going to do?" she cried.

A kind voice answered her. "Now what seems to be the trouble, kids?"

May looked up from Munchlax to see an older woman with gray hair. She wore an orange dress with a white apron over it.

"My Munchlax is feeling really sick and I don't know what to do," May explained.

"Sakes! What a shame," the woman said, shaking her head. She walked up to Munchlax and put her hand on his forehead. "That is *some* fever! But I'm sure I can help."

"Oh, thank you!" May said gratefully.

Then an older man walked up. He had a gray mustache. He wore a red hat on his head and blue suspenders over his white shirt. He carried a wicker basket on his back.

"Is there a problem?" the man asked.

"Sure is, Pa!" said the gray-haired woman. "This here Munchlax is feelin' mighty puny right now."

"Then let's hustle. *I'll* take care of it!" the man said. He pounded his chest with confidence.

As he spoke, a small pink Pokémon popped out of the basket. It had a round, pink nose. When the man moved, the Pokémon copied his motions.

"Hey, it's Mime Jr.!" Brock cried.

"Awesome," Ash said. He loved meeting new Pokémon. He took out his Pokédex. A picture of Mime Jr. appeared on the small screen.

"Mime Jr., the Mime Pokémon," Ash's Pokédex said. "It can quickly imitate anyone it sees. It can sense people's emotions, as well. And when it senses danger, it will erect a barrier so it can escape."

Mime Jr. twirled around on the basket as the Pokédex talked.

For a second, May forgot all about Munchlax. Mime Jr. was so cute!

"Wow, it's darling!" she cooed. Then she came back to her senses. "Oh, Munchlax, what am I saying?"

The older woman turned to her husband. "Quick! Bring Munchlax into the house!" she cried.

L'il James

Not far away, one of the members of Team Rocket was worried, too. James's Pokémon, Chimecho, was feeling sick. James had the Psychic-type Pokémon resting on a bed of leaves.

"Try and relax, Chimecho, please!" James pleaded.

But the Pokémon's little round body tossed and turned. Its long tail thrashed as it moaned softly.

"Meowth, how hard can it be to read a Pokémon Center map?" James snapped.

The talking Pokémon held the map in its paws.

"Oh, dis one's really easy to read cause there ain't nothing on it!" Meowth snapped back.

"What?" James was panicked. He knew his poor Chimecho needed help — fast.

Jessie, his partner in crime, did not seem as worried. "We could use *Heal Bell,* you know," she said.

"That's it!" James cried. Heal Bell was one of Chimecho's moves. The Pokémon could use it in Battle — or whenever it needed — to recover when it was sick or injured. "Chime, go and heal yourself with Heal Bell!"

But all Chimecho could manage was a tiny gasp.

"Chimecho!" James wailed. "The poor dear's too weak to use its own powers! If I don't come up with something soon ..." He held his head in his hands.

"One of your headaches again?" Jessie asked.

Jessie's blue Pokémon, Wobbuffet, popped out of its Poké Ball.

"Wobbuffet!" it cried.

"Will you be quiet!" James yelled. He picked up Chimecho and ran. Chimecho needed help — now!

James ran to the edge of a cliff and looked down. From this high place he could see for miles.

"There's got to be one," he muttered. "I won't stop until I find a Pokémon Center!"

James scanned the land below. Through the trees, he could make out a large building. It looked like a mansion, or maybe a small castle. Towers and turrets jutted up toward the sky.

James gasped. "Could it be?" he breathed. He nodded. "It is!"

James scrambled down the cliff. Jessie and Meowth chased after him.

"Where are you going?" Jessie called out. But James didn't answer her.

Then the building came into view. It didn't look like any Pokémon Center Jessie or Meowth had ever seen.

"They put people in jail for trespassing!" Meowth cried, suddenly nervous.

But James kept running. He ran right under the archway of roses by the front entrance. Then he ran down the wide, stone porch.

An older man and woman came out of the building — the same couple who stopped to help May's Munchlax.

"Nanny! Pop-Pop!" James yelled.

Jessie and Meowth skidded to a stop.

"Nanny?" Jessie asked.

"Pop-Pop?" Meowth added. What was James talking about?

"Hold your Horsea. We're coming," said the older man.

But the woman suddenly smiled. "My, well, if it isn't L'il James!" she cried happily.

James's Secret

"'L'il James!'" Jessie and Meowth were shocked.

James ran up to his Nanny and Pop-Pop. "I'm so glad to see you!" he said.

"Nice to see you, too," said Pop-Pop.

"And in such good health," Nanny added.

James looked at the Chimecho in his arms. "I wish I could say the same for Chimecho," he said sadly.

"Let's have a look," Nanny said. She took the Chimecho from James. The Pokémon gave a little moan.

Pop-Pop nodded. "Yep, something's not right."

"Now don't you worry, Li'l James," Nanny said gently.

Then Pop-Pop noticed Jessie and Meowth at the other end of the porch. "Li'l James? Are those two friends of yours?"

Jessie waved and smiled. "Howdee do, you two!"

"I do remember your ma and pa telling us that you got engaged," Nanny said. "So is she the one? She looks like such a dear!"

James went pale at the thought of marrying Jessie. He imagined Jessie ordering him around: *Clean the house! Cook the food! Take out the garbage!*

Then James snapped out of his daydream. "Jessie's actually my executive secretary," James lied. "And my personal manager is Meowth."

"Secretary?" Jessie asked, annoyed.

"Manager?" Meowth asked.

Nanny was impressed. "Would you listen to the way that Meowth can talk!"

"That's mighty clever, hiring a talking Pokémon

as your manager, young man," Pop-Pop agreed.

"Yeah, mighty clever," Jessie and Meowth said, glaring at James.

"Time out!" James cried. He quickly pulled them aside. They huddled together behind a wide column.

"Okay, so what's the deal?" Jessie whispered.

James sighed. He didn't want to explain this, but he had no choice. "Well, to start with, this is one of my summer cottages."

Jessie couldn't believe it. "You call this a cottage?" Jessie knew James came from a rich family — but this was ridiculous!

"I used to come and visit my Nanny and Pop-Pop every summer when I was small," James went on. "You see, at home, I had a multitude of tutors coming to my house every day for lessons.

Even when I wasn't studying, I was working!" James shuddered at the memory of his childhood. Every move he made was treated like a lesson.

"I couldn't even eat without someone giving me a hard time," James continued. If he held his fork the wrong way, or chewed too loudly, he got scolded.

"And then there were the piano lessons and the violin lessons," James said. "That's why I couldn't wait to come here in the summer. Nanny and Pop-Pop's kindness toward me was a constant, refreshing amazement."

But what James remembered most of all was how kind they were to Pokémon. The house was always filled with Pokémon in need of help.

"Whenever they were faced with an injured Pokémon, they would happily nurse it back to health," James said. "Don't you see? I had to show them what a complete success I've become!"

Jessie and Meowth understood.

"I could see it being a bummer telling them you're a Team Rocket guy," Meowth said. "Well, you can count on us!"

James was surprised. It wasn't like Jessie and Meowth to be helpful.

"But you're going to owe us big-time!" Jessie warned.

James nodded. "Deal!"

Then they heard Nanny's voice. "Something wrong?"

Jessie and Meowth jumped out from behind the column. Jessie smiled brightly. "No way! Nothing beats being executive secretary of the great and powerful James!"

"Being manager's a dream come true!" Meowth added.

"That's nice, but we have a sick Pokémon here," Nanny said, looking down at Chimecho.

James panicked again at the sight of his sick friend. "Nanny, help us!" he cried.

4

"R" Is for "Royalty"

Nanny and Pop-Pop led James and the others through the mansion. They brought Chimecho to a bright, sunny room. They set the Pokémon down on a comfortable bed.

"It looks like the problem here is your Chimecho's exhausted," Pop-Pop explained.

"I'm afraid this poor child needs a good rest," Nanny added.

"Right, Chime?" James asked. He leaned over the bed. Chimecho could not even open its eyes. He let out a worried sigh.

Mime Jr. walked into the room, curious. It stood by James's feet.

Jessie saw the little Pokémon first. "Aw, cutie-pie!" she cried.

James knelt down and greeted Mime Jr. "Hi. The name's James!"

"*Mime!*" the Pokémon said happily.

But Pop-Pop had noticed something. "Would you mind telling me what that 'R' is on your shirt?" he asked.

James almost fainted at the question. But Jessie jumped in front of him. "Why, he's wearing our company uniform!" she said cheerfully. "It's that red 'R' that stands for 'Royalty' and 'Romance'!" She opened her arms wide.

"Yes, she's right again," James said. He nervously rubbed the back of his head. Mime Jr. jumped up on a chair and copied James. "Pretty slick, don't you think?"

"Slick as a wet road!" Pop-Pop agreed.

Nanny wiped a tear from her eye. "Sure know how to make your nanny cry, don't ya, L'il James?"

"Now, don't do that!" James cried, waving his hand.

"*Mime Mime Mime!*" Mime Jr. waved its hand, too.

But Nanny kept crying. "Your ma and pa are going to be so proud of what you've done!"

James held up his arms in surprise. "Are you saying they're here?" he asked in horror. Mime Jr. held up its arms, too.

"Course not. They've been traveling on a world cruise for months now," Nanny replied.

James relaxed. "Gee, what a shame."

Then the doors to the room burst open. Ash, May, Max, and Brock stood there.

"Excuse me, I need some water for my Pokémon," Ash began. He froze when he saw who was in the room.

"Team Rocket!" Ash cried.

5

A Truce

"Twerps!" James yelled, panicked. "Long time no see!"

He ran to the door and quickly shut it behind him.

Ash glared at James. When Team Rocket was around, that could only mean trouble.

"All right, what are you doing here?" Ash asked.

"You watch your step!" Brock warned. "There's a nice old man and woman living here who help injured Pokémon!"

"Will you give it a rest?" James snapped.

Ash and his friends exchanged surprised looks. What was going on?

James dropped to his knees. He began to explain the situation in a whisper. Ash, May, Max, and Brock could not believe what they were hearing.

"It's *your* summer cottage?" Max asked.

"That's your Nanny and Pop-Pop?" Ash asked.

"They took care of you when you were little?" May asked.

"You're telling them you're president of a company that doesn't exist?" Brock asked.

James nodded. "That sums it up pretty well," he said.

"Whoa." The friends still could not believe the story.

"So, I guess that means you're rich," Max remarked.

"Loaded," James said. "But what are you twerps doing here, too?"

"See, my Munchlax was feeling really sick, and

Nanny and Pop-Pop offered to help us," May explained.

"Why am I not surprised?" James said. "So, since we've all ended up here, what do you say we call a truce?"

"What do you mean, truce?" Ash asked.

"I promise I won't do anything nasty while we're here, as long as you guys keep it a secret that I'm in Team Rocket," James said. "I couldn't bear to hurt Nanny and Pop-Pop."

May nodded. "I feel the same way, too!"

"After all they've done for Munchlax, it's the least we can do," Brock agreed.

Nanny opened the door. "Excuse me, L'il James," she said.

James jumped up, startled.

Pop-Pop appeared behind Nanny. "Are all of these young people your friends, too?"

James gave his biggest smile. "Of course! Best friends!"

"He's always chasing us," Max joked.

James quickly put his hand over Max's mouth.

"Cute, huh? Always with the humor. Just like a kid, right?"

"Yep! Just like you when you were a youngster!" Pop-Pop said.

They all went back inside. Nanny and Pop-Pop had moved Munchlax to a bed right next to Chimecho. Both Pokémon were sleeping. Munchlax had stopped moaning and was breathing softly.

"Looks like your Munchlax is feeling much better," Nanny remarked.

May stroked Munchlax's head and smiled. "Thanks to you both," she said gratefully.

"Feel better, Munchlax?" Max asked.

"*Munchlax,*" the Pokémon answered.

James smiled proudly. "When it comes to healing Pokémon, Nanny and Pop-Pop are the tops!" he bragged.

Pop-Pop looked around and scratched his head. "Wonder where your secretary and manager went to?"

James froze. He looked at Ash and the others, and he knew they were thinking the same thing. If Jessie and Meowth were missing, they were up to no good.

"I'll go check," James said quickly.

James ran out of the room, and Mime Jr. followed. They looked all over the mansion. James couldn't find them anywhere.

Then he had an idea.

Mime Jr. followed as James ran to the kitchen. Just as he thought, Jessie and Meowth were kneeling in front of the refrigerator. They were stuffing their faces with food!

James switched on the light. "I should have known," he said. He grabbed his hair in frustration. Mime Jr. grabbed its own head, too. "Where are your manners? That is not your food!"

Jessie and Meowth turned around.

"So what else are you supposed to do when

you're hungry?" Jessie asked. Her mouth was full of carrots.

"Go and paint the house?" Meowth asked.

James pointed at them both, and Mime Jr. copied him. "Stop! You two promised you'd be good!"

"You call this being bad?" Jessie asked.

Nanny, Pop-Pop, and the others appeared at the kitchen door.

"Now what's with all the ruckus?" Pop-Pop asked.

"Uh, my executive secretary and manager were making sure I'd be pleased with the food, nothing more!" James lied.

"You shoulda told me," Nanny said. "I would have made one of your favorites. I know them by heart."

James sighed with relief. Nanny believed his story.

"Say, I've got an idea," Nanny went on. "Why don't you go and show everyone the Pokémon House?"

"Now you're talking!" Pop-Pop said.

James wasn't so sure. Jessie and Meowth would have a hard time staying out of trouble in the Pokémon House. He just hoped they would keep their promise to him.

He had to keep his secret a little while longer!

A Pokémon Paradise!

Nanny and Pop-Pop led everyone to a huge, glass house on the grounds of the mansion. They stepped inside to see a lush, green garden. A waterfall splashed down a hill into a river that wound through the grass.

"It's just like I remember," James said. "Such beauty in its simplicity!"

"We've got all kinds of Pokémon here," Pop-Pop said. He pointed to a tree. A Spinarak dropped down from a web line. An Aipom hung upside down from a tree branch.

"And, of course, there's the Wooper!"

Pop-Pop said proudly. Two little blue Pokémon popped their heads out of the man-made river.

Max and May ran up to them. "They're so cute!" May cooed.

"I'm impressed," Jessie said, looking around at all of the Pokémon.

"This place is a Pokémon paradise!" Meowth agreed.

Just then, an Oddish ran past Jessie and Meowth. It looked like a blue ball with green leaves sticking out of its head. It quickly disappeared into the tall grass.

"Wow, that Oddish can hustle!" Jessie remarked.

"Yep!" Pop-Pop said. "That Oddish was hurt pretty bad when we got ahold of it, but it's fine now."

Jessie and Meowth quietly backed up into the grass.

"Yes, fine for us!" Jessie hissed.

"Primo Pokémon for poachin'!" Meowth added.

The two Pokémon thieves had a greedy look in their eyes as they walked toward the Oddish. They reached out . . .

"*Oddish!*" the little Pokémon squeaked.

James ran through the grass. "What was that?" he asked. "Is something wrong?"

Jessie quickly held the Oddish behind her back. "Oh, things

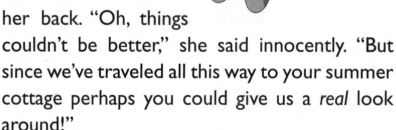

couldn't be better," she said innocently. "But since we've traveled all this way to your summer cottage perhaps you could give us a *real* look around!"

James noticed some leaves sticking up behind Jessie's head.

"Where did you get that?" he asked.

"Oh this? I'm going to plant a tree," Jessie lied.

The Oddish jumped on top of Jessie's shoulder. James frowned.

"It's growing already," he said.

Jessie held the Oddish. It glared at her with angry red eyes.

"An Oddish, wow!" she said. "I thought something was tickling my back!"

James plucked the Oddish from Jessie's arms. He gently placed it on the ground, and it ran away.

Now it was James's turn to glare at Jessie.

"You promised!" James hissed. "No funny stuff!"

"I can't help it if that Oddish wanted to have funzies with me," Jessie said. "And such a cutie wootie!"

James sighed. Jessie would never change!

But James did not worry about Jessie for long. His Chimecho was still sick. When night came, James sat in a chair next to Chimecho's bed.

Mime Jr. walked into the room. It frowned when it saw James's sad face.

Then May walked in. She headed for Munchlax's bed.

"I was worried about Munchlax," she told James.

"Munchlax is asleep," James told her. "I know everything is going to be just fine."

"I sure hope you're right," May said.

"Besides, I'll stay here tonight and keep an eye on things," James added.

"So how's your Chimecho doing?" May asked.

"A little better, I think," James said, giving Chimecho a worried look. "It's my fault. I shouldn't have brought Chimecho this far."

"I'm sorry," May said softly.

"But don't worry about a thing!" James told her. "You just get yourself some sleep."

May nodded. "I will. Thank you!" She bent down and kissed Munchlax on the forehead. "Sleep well, Munchlax!"

May quietly left the room. Mime Jr. ran up to James, waving its hands.

"Mime! Mime Mime Mime!" it said.

James understood the little Pokémon. "Really? You want to be my nurse's aid?"

Mime Jr. nodded. *"Mime Mime Mime!"*

James smiled. "You know what? I think you're awfully sweet."

But while Mime Jr. was being helpful, Jessie and Meowth were up to no good. The pair was sneaking around the mansion with a flashlight. And they had a plan.

Jessie looked at Meowth and grinned. "You can keep trouble out of Team Rocket..."

"But ya can't keep Team Rocket outta trouble!" Meowth cried.

7

Thieves in the Night

James fell asleep with his head resting on Chimecho's bed. Mime Jr. leaned against James's arm and slept, too.

Jessie and Meowth quietly crept into the room.

"Sleep, my L'il James," Jessie whispered. "Dream on."

"While you get some shut-eye, we'll get busy!" Meowth said. He threw a blanket over Mime Jr.

Jessie pushed Munchlax into a big sack. "First we bag Munchlax and Mime Jr., too ..."

chapter
7

"Then the whole Pokémon House crew!" Meowth finished.

They tiptoed out of the room.

In another part of the mansion, Ash stirred in his sleep. He rubbed his eyes and sat up. Something was wrong. He could feel it.

Ash walked to the window. He could see a light shining through the glass walls of the Pokémon House.

"Hey, something's up!" he cried.

James woke up at the same time, too. He looked around, confused.

"Mime Jr., where are you?" he asked. "And where's Munchlax? It's way too late for a midnight snack!"

James glanced out the window. He saw the light in the Pokémon House, too.

"What's that?" he wondered.

The light was Jessie and Meowth's flashlight, of course. They walked through the house, scooping up every Pokémon they could find.

Whoosh! Spinarak went into the sack.

Whoosh! Aipom went into the sack.

Whoosh! The two little Wooper went into the sack.

Whoosh! Oddish went into the sack.

Jessie and Meowth carried the sack full of Pokémon through the glass house. Then, suddenly, the lights went on.

"Team Rocket!" Ash cried. Pikachu, Max, Brock, and May stood with him.

"Where do you think you're going with those Pokémon?" May demanded.

Jessie grinned and began the Team Rocket motto.

"Prepare for trouble, we're going anywhere we please!" she said.

Then James popped up behind her. "And make it double; this stuff is a breeze!"

"An evil as old as the galaxy," Jessie said.

"Sent here to fulfill our destiny," James continued.

"With Meowth to ..." Meowth began, but then James came to his senses.

"Okay, time-out!" he yelled. "Do I have to remind you that you promised to behave your bad selves?"

Jessie looked surprised. "Asking us to behave is like asking a baby not to cry!"

"And we're babies, all right," Meowth said.

James grabbed the huge sack of Pokémon. "Give me that!"

"In your dreams!" Jessie shot back. She would not let go.

Meowth grabbed the sack, too. "I worked my tail off trapping them!" it protested.

"And you're proud of that?" James asked.

James, Jessie, and Meowth tugged and pulled on the sack.

Rrrrrrrrrrrrrip! The sack tore open, and the kidnapped Pokémon scampered out.

"What? They took Munchlax, too?" May asked in disbelief.

"How dare you!" James yelled at his friends. He put his hands on his hips, and Mime Jr. copied him. "Have you no shame?"

Jessie glared at James. "*You* prepare for trouble!" she yelled. "Seviper, let's go!"

8

James vs. Team Rocket

Jessie threw a Poké Ball, and her Poison-type Pokémon popped out. Seviper had a long, snakelike body. Two sharp fangs jutted from its mouth.

"Phanpy, I choose you!" Ash yelled. A small, blue Pokémon with a long trunk exploded from a Poké Ball.

"Seviper, Poison Tail!" Jessie cried.

Seviper lashed out with its tail.

"Rollout, Phanpy, now!" Ash commanded.

Phanpy began to roll across the grass.

Slam! It crashed into Seviper at high speed. Seviper went flying backward.

James threw a Poké Ball next. "Cacnea, let's go!"

A round, green Pokémon came out of the ball. It had stubby arms and legs. Sharp spikes grew out of its body. It faced off against Ash's Phanpy.

"Not them!" James yelled. "Seviper's the object of your affliction now!"

Cacnea looked confused. It had never been asked to battle Seviper before. Jessie was furious.

"You traitor!" she yelled.

"What are you doin', siding with the twerps?" Meowth asked.

"I'm *siding* with Nanny and Pop-Pop!" James said. "Cacnea, use Sandstorm!"

Cacnea raised its arms, and a wind kicked up in front of it. The wind traveled toward Seviper until it became a spinning tornado of sand.

"Some Sandstorm!" May said.

"Use Wrap, Seviper!" Jessie urged.

Seviper raced toward Cacnea.

"Cacnea, use Needle Arm, go!" James cried.

Seviper slammed into Cacnea, but Cacnea hit Seviper with its spike-filled arm. The attack sent Seviper reeling.

James turned to Ash. "Now twerp, your turn!"

Ash nodded. "You got it! Phanpy, Hidden Power!"

Phanpy raised its trunk. Bright white light shot out, hitting Jessie, Meowth, and Seviper.

"Cacnea, Pin Missile!" James cried.

Cacnea sent a shower of sharp spikes at

Jessie, Meowth, and Seviper. The combination of the two attacks sent Team Rocket flying.

"There's nothing worse than getting your head handed to you by a friend!" Jessie moaned.

"No duh," Meowth said.

"And we're blasting off again!" Jessie and Meowth screamed.

Then they flew out of the open roof and vanished into the night sky.

Nanny and Pop-Pop ran into the Pokémon House.

"Now what are you doing up at all hours of the night?" Pop-Pop asked.

James grinned sheepishly. "I guess I was reliving my childhood and playing with my Pokémon," he said.

"That sounds great!" May said, playing along.

"Playing with Pokémon is fun, don't you think?" Ash asked.

"Sure!" Brock agreed.

"Pika!" Pikachu added.

Nanny smiled warmly. "It does a heart good to see all these young people here," she said.

Pop-Pop looked around. "But your secretary and manager sure can't stay in one place at all."

Just then, Jessie and Meowth came crashing back down. They landed with a thud next to Nanny and Pop-Pop.

"Were you two taking care of business?" Nanny asked.

"A secretary's work is never done!" Jessie said.

"But we've always got time to drop in," Meowth added.

James smiled. It looked like this story would end happily. Except . . .

"Chimecho," James whispered sadly.

Good-bye and Hello

9

The next morning, Ash, May, Max, and Brock were ready to go on their way. Nanny and Pop-Pop stood by the front door to see them off.

"Munchlax has got that famous appetite back and feels great, thanks to you," May said.

"Well, we're glad that we could help," Pop-Pop replied.

"We sure do hope everything goes your way at the Battle Arena, Ash," Nanny said.

"Thanks! Take care!" Ash said, waving.

"Pika! Pika!" Pikachu waved, too.

"You take good care of yourself!" Pop-Pop called out as the friends walked away.

"And take care of each other!" Nanny added.

Meanwhile, on the roof of the mansion, Jessie and Meowth waited in Team Rocket's balloon.

"James is late again," Jessie whined.

"What else is new?" Meowth asked. "I wonder what he's messin' with this time?"

James was sitting at Chimecho's side. He knew he had to leave. But he couldn't leave Chimecho like this!

Then the Pokémon opened its eyes. It gave James a weak smile.

"Chime!" James cried happily.

Nanny and Pop-Pop walked in with Mime Jr. at their feet.

"James, I'm afraid this baby's going to have to stay here," Nanny said.

"But Nanny, I've got to get going, and I won't leave without Chimecho," James said.

"But if we move Chimecho too soon, it could be dangerous," Pop-Pop pointed out.

James's eyes started to fill with tears. "Of course I know this is serious," he said. "It's just that ... I don't know how to deal with this. I love my Chimecho!"

James thought of all the happy times he had with his Pokémon. Chimecho used to wrap its long, flat tail around James's face. The sweet Pokémon had always made James laugh.

James choked back tears. He knew leaving Chimecho with Nanny and Pop-Pop was the best thing. But he would miss Chimecho so much!

A tear rolled down his cheek and splashed on Chimecho's face. The little Pokémon was crying now, too.

"Chime!" James sobbed.

Mime Jr. looked up at James, worried.

James wiped his tears with his sleeve. He turned to Nanny and Pop-Pop.

"Take care of Chime, will you?" he asked.

"Course we will!" Pop-Pop promised.

"Just like one of our own babies," Nanny said.

James reached into his pocket. "Let me give you Chimecho's Poké Ball."

Several tiny Poké Balls spilled from his pocket. One of the balls dropped to the floor. It expanded to its real size.

Mime Jr. grinned when it saw the Poké Ball. With a happy cry, it ran toward it.

"Mime! Mime!"

James watched, shocked, as the Poké Ball emitted a red light. Mime Jr. disappeared inside the ball.

"Mime Jr.?" James asked. "What just happened?"

"It's looking to me like you just found yourself a good buddy in Mime Jr.," Pop-Pop said.

"Good buddy?" James asked.

"Mime Jr. has an amazing way of picking up on people's emotions, and could tell you were feeling kind of lonely and pretty scared right now," Nanny explained. "Why don't you take along your new friend?"

"*Chime,*" Chimecho smiled happily. James knew Chimecho approved. He reached down and picked up the Poké Ball.

Nanny and Pop-Pop had done so much for them. He owed them something.

The truth.

James took a deep breath. "Before we go, I've got something to tell you both ..."

A little while later, Nanny and Pop-Pop watched Team Rocket's balloon fly up into the sky. James waved down to them.

"I still can't believe our L'il James got all mixed up with that Team Rocket," Pop-Pop said.

"Me neither, but he's still the same sweetheart he was when he was just a little boy," Nanny said. "And it looks like he's found some good friends — friends that are looking after him, too. So it really doesn't matter what they call themselves, now does it? After all, he's gonna be who he's gonna be!"

Pop-Pop nodded. "And as long as he's happy then I am, too."

Nanny grinned. "Right!"

James kept waving until Nanny and Pop-Pop were out of sight. He looked down at the Poké Ball in his hand.

Leaving Chimecho behind was hard. But it helped to have a new friend, Mime Jr. And of course, Chimecho would always be in his heart.

And so will the happy little boy called L'il James, he thought with a smile.